RECKLESS ABANDON

JARED FELDSCHREIBER

CONTENTS

AUTHOR'S NOTE

It was my intention to be as *truthful* as I could while writing *Reckless Abandon*. Granted, *truthfulness* within literature can be ambiguous, but to coalesce true events, and *truthful* passages with the supposed "what if" imaginary realm felt right all along. It is a device that my literary heroes like Norman Mailer, David Mamet, Woody Allen, and Bob Dylan, have implemented within their works, and with far greater success.

My strategy for *Reckless Abandon* was to put in all of the necessary legwork, such as spending afternoons at the New York Public Library retrieving microfilm of old newspaper clippings. I also watched repeatedly footage of sports and news events depicted in the narrative, and took day tours in New York, like to Madison Square Garden, Museum of the City of New York City, Brooklyn Historical Society, as well as stopping by the Syracuse Stage and the

Broadhurst Theatre. I am not an authority of New York's literary or cultural history, but at least these efforts reflect a *truthful* attempt of authenticity. I sought to consistently match the milieu with the zeitgeist of the time, specifically in the summer of 1984.

I omitted a huge chunk of what it might've been like *actually* in Manhattan, Syracuse, or near Dublin in 1984, but I essayed to the best of my creative abilities what it would've been like *experientially*. John Duggan is not my alter ego, or a piece of my autobiography, but his yearnings may be, regardless of the time and place. Many of the quotations I culled from the cultural heroes in this novella were *actual* comments they made at some point during the course of their careers. But, again, the dialogue sprung from my imagination.

I am grateful to family and friends who read, re-read, and in some cases, sent me their copious notes, or made sideline suggestions, in an effort to make the narrative not just more coherent, but also making *Reckless Abandon* a more compelling read.

Thank you Gabrielle Harradine for her editing prowess, as well as Austin Arrington, Maksym Bilousiv, Philippe Brunot, Michael Gerber, Dan Hyman, Ryan Lefkowitz, and others for reading all or snippets of prior drafts. Each helped me fill in the gaping holes within the narrative. Thank you, too, Justyna Miklasiewicz for her invaluable help with the cover design and her overall artistic sensibilities. Above all, thank you to my parents. I hope I have done them proud with this novella, and I will always love them so very much. They will forever be the touchstones of my life.

Jared Feldschreiber
May 2019

"I'm a Brooklyn-Broadway wisecracker who's been very lucky."
- Woody Allen

"The name of the game is compromise, once you're successful."
– Dustin Hoffman

"I always admired true artists. So I learned from them."
– Bob Dylan

CHAPTER I

John Duggan, a New York theatre critic and aspiring playwright, just watched a performance of Arthur Miller's *Death of a Salesman,* as directed by Volker Schlöndorff, and starring Dustin Hoffman as Willy Loman. The setting is near the Broadhurst Theatre in late May 1984.

John is seen conversing with his friend Dmitri outside 44th Street in Manhattan. During the question-and-answer session that followed the play, John grew moved by the actor's honesty, as Hoffman interpreted Willy Loman as like his own father who had also been a struggling salesman.

"The reason why I did '*Salesman'* is because of my father," Hoffman told the audience. "He was angry. He was bitter. He was very close to that part, and when he came to see it, he came backstage, and I was nervous for him coming to it. I said, 'What'd you think, Dad?' 'Boy, what a loser that guy is."

This touched John, a critic with further aspirations who had enormous respect for Hoffman as a consummate artist. John grew afraid his own theatrical background would make him merely a critic, a job he loved but was hardly fulfilling. He studied playwriting at SUNY Purchase. He completed a draft of his soon-to-be production – *Reckless Abandon* – and he grew increasingly convinced that his journalistic career would blend in nicely toward being a respected playwright.

John came from a good family, oft-times garnering respect for his perceptive wit within his analyses. He earned great guidance from his parents. After this performance, Duggan wanted his first production to involve his three artistic heroes: Dustin Hoffman, Bob Dylan and Woody Allen.

Around this time, Woody Allen was shooting *The Purple Rose of Cairo* in Piermont, New York, and in recent years, was notorious for shunning most talk shows. It hardly mattered since John always managed to save old clippings of Allen, and amassed VHS recordings, which contained some pertinent details of the making of his films.

Bob Dylan, meanwhile, often ornery around critics, was somewhere in Germany, or perhaps Belgium, or Italy, during the European leg of his tour, selling out to hundreds of thousands. These concerts featured Carlos Santana and Joan Baez, and a host of other special musical guests. After months of collecting checks for his freelance work, John saved up his funds to finally see Dylan.

John managed to get his hands on the last
show of the tour, which took place at Slane
Castle near Dublin. He had every intention
to hand Dylan his script while there. Needless to
say, this was a dream project for John. While his
inner anxieties knew that he hardly measured up
to his cultural heroes, it still would not deter him
– even as he never knew how it would pan out.

John and Dmitri had been friends for
eight years, as both were Theater Arts majors
together at SUNY Purchase. These days Dmitri
worked comfortably in finance, putting his
artistic dreams on the shelf, at least for a few
more years. If ever he got back into "the game"
of theatrical productions, it would certainly be in
financing, as his writing definitely hit "a wall."

"Bobby Dylan is now in Hamburg,
Woody is in Piermont up the Hudson River, and
here's Dustin," John exclaimed to Dmitri as they

enjoyed a smoke outside the Broadhurst Theatre. "How come they've never worked together? I'm going to put together a play to utilize their tremendous talents," John proclaimed.

To his credit, John already wrote a workmanlike draft of *Reckless Abandon* but it was hardly polished. He attempted to speak to management at the Broadhurst earlier in the day, and to pass the script to Hoffman, but to no avail. He thought he saw the actor during Intermission beside one of the bathroom stalls, but even if it were Hoffman, it would not be appropriate to hand him the script then and there.

"John, buddy, it's a great premise," insisted Dmitri. "But where are you going to get the money for this? How are you going to pass all of the legalese, and complicated theatrical bureaucratic mumbo-jumbo?" It was almost as if Dmitri was subliminally goading John to hire him. "Hate to tell you but I'm just not sure you can climb this mountain. These guys have agents. Their agents have agents. It's an intriguing pie-in the sky-dream, but you know that pie may just be too high in the sky."

"Dim – I know but I just feel the energy. I'll put the legwork in, and do even more research. I feel like Bernard King on the open break. It's like when he swoops in for his patented finger roll. Remember last month during the Pistons-Knicks playoff game when Isiah scored 16 points in 93 seconds? It still wasn't enough to get past King and the Knicks, and they played in that sauna."

Dmitri, a diehard Knicks fan, just nodded.

"When Dylan came to New York, he basically was running away from his upper-middle class Jewish home in Duluth. *I want to feel that journey too.* I even read he cut a deal with his parents. 'Give me six months and see how it goes,' he told them. Read about it in the *Village Voice.*"

"And Woody – He's Allan Stewart Konigsberg from Flatbush born to Orthodox Jews," he continued. "Look at those two – Woody and Bob, so original, and so prolific. And Hoffman? You heard him today as he was practically in tears. He took his father's failure to personify Willy Loman. It'll no doubt win him the Drama Desk Award, but more than anything else, it came from a *truthful* place."

"I see. John, it's intriguing. But where will you do this? Syracuse Stage? That's the home of many stage productions."

"Brilliant, Dmitri," responded John.

"What?"

"Syracuse! Hadn't even thought of that."

"Syracuse Stage isn't really a rental house, as far as I know, and even if you could, it'll cost you."

"Well, this project is within me somehow. It just comes from a *truthful* place. It's not like

Reagan's 'Morning in America' cockamamie ads. Maybe you'll be my production manager?"

"Just let me know how I can help," Dmitri said with a smile and took a beat. "You know this somewhat reminds me of the Paul Mazurksy film that came out recently with Robin Williams – what was that called? *Moscow on the Hudson?*"

"Yeah, so?"

"That film is about a struggling artist – a struggling foreigner – but in the literal sense. It's as if you're the foreigner for the life of the artist, and you're peeking in, in some kind of way."

"That's interesting, Dmitri – never thought of it that way. Your way of thinking is so atypical, but brilliant."

Dmitri just rolled his eyes, but again elicited a slight smile. "I hope this project takes off. It's a worthy exploration that speaks to your soul, so block out the naysayers who aren't behind it. Take their criticism, or take their jealousy, wisely."

"You're a good friend, Dmitri," said John. "Am just not sure how to get directly to Bob, Woody and Dustin. I could perhaps meet Woody on the set in Piermont, and I did save up for the Dylan show outside Dublin. It's just that with this new boom in the economy – we're three years into Reagan – I wonder if there's a place for this type of artistic exploration."

"There's always a place. Gotta believe that."

"Do I present myself as producer or as director or as playwright?

"Doesn't matter; you're the creator."

"Thanks, D."

CHAPTER II

John got back to his Lower Manhattan digs, a modest place, but not by any means a squalid dump. In 1984, it was popular for those trying to break into the theatrical world to live in sub-apartments, as they were called. Some would just be offered a room in someone else's apartment.

At least John had his own place.

In his creative works that he never published, John always depicted his protagonists as *purveyors of truth.* It was a motif he picked up from Woody Allen. It also seeped into his literary journalistic works. He made his living as a freelancer, largely writing theatre reviews with *The Brooklyn Eagle*, and occasionally *The Daily News and New York Herald.* He wrote some biographies in *Playbill,* as well. This included a detailed piece for *Death of a Salesman*, which featured Hoffman alongside up-

and-coming talent John Malkovich, and veritable
stage actress Kate Reid. The opening date of the
play premiered on March 29, 1984, and the run
lasted through the autumn months. John, though,
never summoned up the courage to interview the
performers during the theatrical season.

Dmitri, while John's good friend, still had
an air of mystery. It appeared as though his
theatrical aspirations were dead. He worked with
his uncle as a paralegal and yet he often fancied
himself as a modern-day Anton Chekhov. He
bemoaned that his true passions were stymied by
the realities of the rough-and-tumble New York
City rat race. He was a realist but always
maintained a dreamer's heart, and he somewhat
envied John since his friend had his family's
moral support guiding his artistic dreams.

In the business sector, Dmitri was
uniformly excellent with numbers, and knew
how to deal with all types of analyses. He could

also read the complicated facets of the stock market well. On the ethical scale, he never tried to cut corners either.

After Dmitri graduated from SUNY Purchase in the same year as John, he had his aspirations dashed when *KGB Surprise*, his satirical off-Broadway play of the Reagan era, tanked. His production dealt with KGB agents infiltrating the State Department but who did it for the *right* reasons. It spoke to the commonalities of the two sides. Dmitri used the repeated motif of an empty milk carton to reflect how each country needed the other. It was highly misunderstood but embraced by some critics as being "unique," "perceptive," and "timely." It still lost a ton of money, and his artistic dreams were crushed.

John loved the play, watching it multiple times, and encouraged others to see it. He touted *KGB Surprise* in *The Brooklyn Eagle* as a "worthy exploration to the psychological motivation of Soviets. We are grateful for Dmitri Ivanov's incisive and needed satire," wrote Duggan. While Dmitri would not attempt to produce another play, he privately scribbled story ideas for future plays on loose sleeve pages, and stuck them within his desk drawers.

CHAPTER III

Bob Dylan, the mercurial and reclusive music superstar, began his 1984 summer tour with Carlos Santana, Joan Baez, and Mick Taylor. Rumors circulated that there lay tension in the Dylan-Baez camp, so much so that she was abandoning the tour altogether. Apparently she felt slighted that her billing was reduced on the marquee, and Dylan barely allowed her to join him on stage. John also read that the tour brought back some painful memories for her, as Dylan behaved in a similar fashion two decades earlier.

The roving minstrel alienated some fans in recent years with his foray into Gospel music, but he also retained his base especially as his latest LP, *Infidels,* soared. Dylan's mystic poetry melded perfectly with Mark Knopfler's supreme guitar sound. The leading Dire Straits frontman co-produced the album. Dylan, though, remained a most inscrutable, yet fascinating, performing artist.

For John, *Reckless Abandon* would be his first literary published work. On this evening, John needed ideas to generate some traction to jumpstart his production. He looked up in the White Pages and found Alvin Dexter, a local events promoter who occasionally put on concerts and boxing matches at the Felt Forum, the famed arena just adjacent to Madison Square Garden. Dexter would be the point of contact connecting him with Irving Mitchell Felt, the businessman who led to the construction of Madison Square Garden in the early 1970s.

Felt became president of the Madison Square Garden Corporation when it purchased the New York Knicks and New York Rangers franchises. It dawned on Duggan that Allen, Hoffman and Dylan attended the "Fight of the Century," which pitted Muhammad Ali and Joe Frazier on March 8, 1971. This match was seen as the first big sporting event of the '70s, and just ten months subsequent to the New York Knicks capturing the NBA title, also held at Madison Square Garden.

John was 16 years old when the "Fight of the Century" took place, and while he was not much of a boxing fan, he and his father would routinely speak about it for years. He admired the sports reporter Mark Kram who covered boxing extensively in *Sports Illustrated.* Before contacting Dexter, John rummaged through his drawers to find some of Kram's old clippings.

Kram, one of the most lyrical sportswriters of the '60s and '70s, wrote, "I always wanted to write like Edward Hopper painted." Kram showed the type of 'reckless abandon' John Duggan emphasized in his own work.

John made his way to the New York Public Library to retrieve some of Kram's articles about the match. Duggan also checked out Norman Mailer's *The Fight,* the literary nonfiction work chronicling Ali's upset of

George Foreman in Kinshasa, Zaire in October 1974, better known as the 'Rumble in the Jungle.'

> *"It is not uncommon for fighters' camps to be gloomy,"* wrote Mailer. *"In heavy training, fighters live in dimensions of boredom others do not begin to contemplate. Fighters are supposed to. The boredom creates an impatience with one's life ... Boredom creates a detestation for losing."*

John called Dmitri, realizing his friend had some degree of pull in the city to help with arranging for a meeting with Felt. He scratched his initial plan to call Alvin Dexter himself.

The phone rang twice before Dmitri answered.

"Hello?"

"Hey, I'm just going through some writer's *stuff*. Just wanted to throw some ideas off you; am feeling a bit depressed."

"What gives?" Dmitri asked in his imitable Russian accent that strongly attempted to be American.

"Just feel somewhat down. It's this whole 'meta' thing going on with this play prep. It's too self-reflexive. Plays should be universal in narrative, tone, texture, and attitude."

"I hear you John, but you needn't lament," offered Dmitri. "Get out of your existential rut. You're behaving like Gogo in *Godot*. Just quit the procrastination. You've read Bellow's *Seize the Day*?"

"Of course!"

"Well Wilhelm never did 'seize the day.' That was his Achilles' heel. Do your research, conduct the interviews, and see it through. You'll be fine. I assume there's another reason why you called me?"

"Yeah, well, with your connections, would you mind getting in touch with the top brass over at the Garden? Very much would like to speak to Irving Mitchell Felt."

"Sure. I'll call you in the morning after it's arranged."

By the next morning, the meeting had been set.

John headed to the Felt Forum seeking more information about the impresario who built the structure. He read a few billboards off to the side of the venue, wanting to discover more about the epic Ali-Frazier bout. Mailer was there, as was Frank Sinatra, and so of course were Allen, Dylan and Hoffman.

Irving Mitchell Felt was a highly successful businessman who led the initiative for building Madison Square Garden on West 33rd Street. It was under Felt's direction as president of the Madison Square Corporation when the Rangers and Knicks sports clubs were bought, in addition to the Roosevelt Raceway on Long Island and Holiday on Ice Productions. He was a confident and proud elderly man.

The Ali-Frazier match went on to gross more than $1.3 million, John discovered. He marveled that the event truly was a spectacle with the lure to attract so many luminaries, like Allen, Hoffman and Dylan.

In large part due to Dmitri's wheeling-and-dealing, John secured his interview with Felt. John underscored to Felt's secretary that he was doing research on the history of New York's famous buildings for a story in *The Brooklyn Eagle*, which was partly true.

John found it unique Frank Sinatra opted to work as a ringside photojournalist on the sidelines for the "Fight of the Century" after he was unable to nab a good seat. Sinatra took many of the photographs for *Life* magazine, which published just a few weeks later in its special edition coverage of the match.

Before picking out his attire for his interview, John put on a videocassette recording of the telecast. He listened intently to the sportscaster's introduction of Ali and Frazier.

"Hundreds of millions are seeing this bout around the world. A packed house at Madison Square Garden: Muhammad Ali in the red trunks, [and] Joe Frazier in the green."

While picking out his attire for the meeting, Kris Kristofferson's 'Sunday Morning Coming Down' began to play on the radio.

'Fumbled in my closet through my clothes
And found my cleanest dirty shirt
Then I washed my face and combed my hair
And stumbled down the stairs to meet the day'

John rushed to the Madison Square Garden offices, and he felt buoyant as he shook hands with the business tycoon.

"Thank you for meeting with me, Mr. Felt," he said without showing any sort of nervousness that besieged him for days. John Duggan took comfort in realizing he was his own producer.

"Mr. Duggan," Felt politely responded.
"Why did you come see me this afternoon? And
by the way, you can call me Irving, and please let
me call you John, is it?"

"Yes."

"There it is, then," said Felt who looked
sharp, but with a slight air of displeasure since he
was taken away from his busy schedule.

"Well Irving, I'm hoping to put on this
play. It's more like a medley that features some
of my favorite American cultural heroes."

"Who are these cultural heroes, as you
call them?"

"It's a play involving Bob Dylan, Woody
Allen, and Dustin Hoffman. Thirteen years ago,
they were spectators for the 'Fight of the
Century."

"Ah yes – with Ali and Smokin' Joe –
that was a great night for us. We made a fortune.
It really changed the concept of what's perceived

to be a sports spectacle, if you can call it that."

"Yes, of course. You have quite the track record, sir."

"Thank you son; indeed we do. But why are you coming to me?"

"I just wanted to gain some insight as to how to put together a spectacle like this. I doubt bringing Madison Square Garden out of the ashes, and building it just beside Penn Station was a small feat."

"You're a bit wet behind the ears. Not a bad thing, not a bad thing at all. You're a creative talent. I can see that. Coming to me – within the financial world – you're definitely in a league of sharks. Here you'll just find merely businessmen who care about the bottom line. You know this type of project would be better served up by speaking to an artistic director in Upstate New York. Maybe like at a repertory company at say… Syracuse Stage?

"It's funny you should say that. My friend told me I should speak to someone there."

Felt proceeded to speak in grandiose terms about his successes. "Not everyone was happy with me early on. Granted when I was still about your age, I purchased controlling interest in the old Madison Square Garden, and I wanted to replace the old Garden with a new and modern facility that was more flexible, which could handle larger crowds, and provide unobstructed views."

John noticed that he was dealing with a *true* mogul.

"So, by November 1960, I purchased from the Pennsylvania Railroad the rights to build at Penn Station. In the next summer, I announced the demolition of it, and went on to building what we see today – the modern day Madison Square Garden." Felt displayed various banners on his wall, exhibiting his owned franchises. The Ringling Bros. Circus was the most successful event at the Garden, but Felt lamented of the hype surrounding it each year.

"It was just the pits," he said. "Those elephants are cute but they are laborious to get through the turnstiles, if you know what I mean?"

Duggan did not understand, but still gave a slight smile, knowing he was dealing with a shrewd, talented – if a bit eccentric – capitalist.

"From 1960 to 1968, I oversaw the project from demolition to completion, and it was privately financed. I said at the time that 'the gain from the new buildings and sport center would more than offset any aesthetic loss.' I also predicted that 'fifty years from now, when it's time for Madison Square Garden to be torn down, there will be a new group of architects who will protest.' History will probably prove me right, or maybe it won't."

"What was your best memory in the past 15 years?"

"It really was the Ali-Frazier bout. It's not just because of its thrilling ending with Frazier coming out on top, but for its sheer spectacle. It transcended sport and played within the zeitgeist of the political and cultural milieu of the day. Didn't you see the playoffs last month? Bernard King was a *showman* here. Ali and Frazier were *showmen*. Now we have events here at the Felt Forum where fathers come with their sons, paying good money to watch live boxing matches on closed circuit TV. That fight, though, in '71, really brought the city together."

John could not agree more as the disaffected youth and "the Establishment" were at each other's throats under the Nixon Administration in '71, and for those few hours, this "sports spectacle" brought some needed unity. Ali's fight was his first in three years since being banned from the sport for his opposition to the Vietnam War. Boxing fans universally admired the tenacity, integrity, and skill of Ali and Frazier.

"I don't mean to interrupt you Irving, but did you get to see, or perhaps even say anything to Mr. Allen or Mr. Hoffman when they walked through the turnstiles, or during the match?"

"Ha, what an innocent question! You mean did I see Hoffman or Woody order a hot dog from the concession stand?"

John chose to not smile at Felt's quip.

"Obviously I didn't. But they are regulars at the Garden for Knick games as I'm sure you know," Felt said. "I do see the nexus, though, in what you're doing. They are linked in an intrinsic way far beyond just loving New York sports. Your initiative is a good one."

"Thank you, sir."

"You're an artist, but not a businessman," Felt said as if preparing to make his closing remarks. "I'm the opposite. You needn't forget that. Who knows, maybe they will name an amphitheater here after me? Maybe they won't. My legacy is to bring in all walks of life here for special events."

It was then that John went again from comfort to confusion. He found Irving Mitchell Felt to be a 'can do' type of entrepreneur. John did not look down upon those in the business world, but he could not suppress his dreamlike nature either. He appreciated the interview, gaining new knowledge of the city he loved. He also felt a tingling sensation run up-and-down his leg since he managed to transform himself into the role as producer.

John walked the New York streets confidently, knowing he scored the ultimate interview with a most seminal figure of the city's lore, akin to Robert Moses, even if the "master builder" had many people who reviled him.

While reading a local newspaper, John noticed a few advertisements of the various acting classes offered at the Syracuse Stage. He found a phone number of its esteemed artistic director Arthur Storch, and dialed it. Before long, John set up a meeting with Storch for an informal tour of the playhouse.

John only *knew* of the Syracuse Stage from cinema. One scene in Sydney Pollack's *Tootsie* stood out. It featured Hoffman's character Michael Dorsey and his agent George, as played by director Pollack. The scene satirized Hoffman's reputation as a theatrical perfectionist. His conduct often maddened producers and agents. *"No one will hire you"* was the memorable line.

The Syracuse Stage remained Central New York's premier professional theatre founded in 1974. It produced a sundry of noted performances by luminaries like Sam Waterston, Ben Gazzara, and others. John prepared some questions for personnel there concerning what went into those successful productions. Within a week, John was off to Syracuse.

John loved to replay some of TV host Dick Cavett's best interviews from the 1970s. Just before falling asleep, he put on a VHS recording of one of Cavett's discussions with Woody Allen.

"I exist more happily in my fantasy world than in my real world because I can imagine anything I want in fantasy, and it's a pleasure," Allen told Cavett.

"I was thrown out of NYU, and went to City College. My parents were crushed. I should not be doing comedy. I should be doing Swedish tragedy."

So writing comedy is a talent?

"Writing comedy is a weird talent and I don't think there are too many people that have it."

John already closed his eyes as the TV screen turned blue.

CHAPTER IV

On his ride up to Upstate New York the following Tuesday, John struck up a conversation with an attractive woman from the Upper West Side. Jennifer McClure, coincidentally, was en route to the Syracuse Stage to see a production of Sam Shepard's *True West*. She often rented a guesthouse in the summer months since she routinely bought season tickets. It was a match made in heaven. Her deep understanding of the performing arts impressed John. She often saw films at the Thalia, the famed movie art house in Manhattan. Their repartee soon evolved into a lively discussion about "the role of the artist in cinema."

"I grew up on the Upper West Side, which is why I know about the Thalia," Jennifer said. "I was one of the kids who would help out as an usher. They used to have wall-to-wall composers for twelve hours straight. I was busy handing out flyers. It probably started in '74 or so and went through early '80s," she told him. "I'm now their communications director so it's clearly a lifelong passion, although I would've loved to toil in the artist's life, too. But I've had my fun, as I met Allen, Bogdanovich and Scorsese. They were constantly coming to these foreign films by Felini, Antonioni, Kurosawa, and more."

Their conversation veered to debating why Hoffman and Allen had not worked together up to that point. Both were charmed by one another's perceptive wits, chuckling about all kinds of 'what ifs' and 'maybes.'

"I do think in that late '70s period when Dustin was the 'it' guy, they really should've worked together. Hoffman often went un-credited for writing and directing some things," said John.

For anyone else on the bus, the conversation was a meaningless exercise in artistic pontification. There were far more substantial happenings in the world – the economy, war in the Middle East, or rampant crime in Mayor Ed Koch's New York City, among them.

"But if Woody Allen had directed Hoffman, people would have had trouble distinguishing whose film that they were talking about," said Jennifer. "Is it a Woody Allen movie or was it a Dustin Hoffman movie?"

"There was a movie that Dustin Hoffman turned down of Woody's, I'm not sure what it was; it may have been from the early '70s. Would have been interesting," insisted John.

When John and Jennifer exited the bus, she offered him a drink at her place, and he accepted. The couple consummated their relationship, and spent a good evening together. Above all, they really liked, and respected each other's company and ideas.

On the following morning as the two exchanged numbers, she reminded him to call her when things were ripe for starting the production. Jennifer also gave John a few other contacts in the local theater community, including Don Buschmann, the director of production operations at the Syracuse Stage.

John received an informal tour of the venue later that morning, and had his opportunity to speak with Arthur Storch, the famed director and founder of the facility. Storch appeared punchy at first, clearly rattled by the upcoming evening's show. He was not impressed by Duggan's disposition either.

"There was a major renovation done lately," Storch said with an air of pomposity in his tone. "Here we have a proscenium style stage. I don't mean to brag but we've had a lot of folks from New York City come up here in recent months. It's a home away from Broadway for many known performers. Frank Langella put on a show here recently." John was informed the stage housed four hundred and ninety-nine people.

"We're lucky since the balcony is relatively shallow so you don't need as much support for the people underneath," added Storch. "It's that typical wide but shallow feel so everything feels intimate where you're seated."

While impressed with the facility, and with aspirations to put on his dream project there, John grew impatient by Storch's rote tour on the importance of stage design. He was itching to get to Piermont, and see Woody Allen direct his latest film.

CHAPTER V

When John got home, he listened to a voicemail left by Dmitri.

"Hey, not sure where you are, but we should meet. Answer your phone. Let's meet by Gem Spa at 7:00."

John would practically do anything for Dmitri, a unique first generation Russian émigré turned all-American guy, who always wore his Bernard King t-shirt on his off days. Dmitri worked hard, and looked sharp in his duds, but he still missed "the Motherland."

"In some ways, it's easier here, and I love basketball, and the women here, but I can't say it's better," he often said. While in school, Dmitri double-majored in Business Management so he had a fallback plan, in case that would be needed.

It was.

John played *Damn the Torpedoes,* the
Tom Petty and the Heartbreakers album, on his
audiocassette player. He loved Petty's quick-
witted lyricism, blending Dylan's sense of
brevity coupled with ironic detachment. Rumors
circulated in the media that they were planning
a tour together in another year or so, as Dylan
long admired the younger rock star.

'Somewhere, somehow
Somebody must've kicked you around some
Tell me why you want to lay there
And revel in your abandon
Honey, it don't make no difference to me baby
Everybody's had to fight to be free you see
You don't have to live like a refugee'

John, of course, did not have to "live like
a refugee." *His moment was now.* Even so, he
often sat alone – just reflecting – and to "revel in
[his own] abandon."

John had a fleeting thought that the
Brooklyn Bridge should also be a prevailing
motif in his production. He had a beautiful

framed photograph of the iconic bridge hanging on his wall. The picture included the adage:

"The bridge personified beauty with its long, uninterrupted span extending over the open sea, and the skyscrapers of Manhattan across the river"

The Brooklyn Bridge contained enormous granite towers and steel cables, which connected the boroughs of Brooklyn and Manhattan across the East River with its main span of four hundred and eighty-six meters. It was once one of the world's largest suspension bridges, and extended slightly over a mile from end to end.

It had been over five years since John graduated from SUNY Purchase, and he knew if he were an artist, he needed to generate results. He was thinking of sneaking into another showing of *Death of a Salesman* at the Broadhurst that Friday or Saturday – but it still was only Thursday, so that was not a viable option. He still had his deadlines to finish, as he always gave workmanlike efforts, which he submitted to his varied publications.

John sought to learn more about Piermont, the tiny village that was incorporated in Rockland County in 1947. Piermont, located north of the hamlet of Palisades, east of Sparkill, and south of Grand View-On-Hudson, lay on the west bank of the Hudson River. He knew Woody Allen already set up for his latest film there. It was the filmmaker's follow-up to *Broadway Danny Rose*. Allen began working with his new muse Mia Farrow three years earlier in *A Midsummer Night's Sex Comedy*. *The Purple Rose of Cairo* would be their third collaboration together. Jeff Daniels, who made his film debut in Milos Forman's *Ragtime*, would co-star in it.

John inserted a VHS recording of another Allen interview in which he dispelled the notion that he may be a creative genius.

"A genius? No," Allen bluntly said. *"Leonardo da Vinci was a genius. Mozart was a genius. A genius is a word in the entertainment world that they use everyday and any person is a genius. I certainly am not. I'm just a person who has talent for fun and I've made movies over the years."*

Upon scouring *The Daily News* to learn more about the making of *The Purple Rose of Cairo*, John discovered that while the exterior scenes were being shot in Piermont, some takes involving Daniels' character Tom, and Farrow's Cecilia, were also being filmed at the Bertrand Island Amusement Park. Allen shut down the Kent Theater.

Before calling Dmitri back, John needed fresh air so he dribbled his basketball up 1st Avenue to Robert Moses Park on 41st St. The playground overlooked the East River. "Parks are the outward symbols of democracy," Robert Moses had once said. The noted builder spent five decades conducting New York public service, and the park was acquired by the city in 1937 as part of the Queens-Midtown Tunnel construction. The same basketball court where John played since he was in third grade was completed in 1941, only for the site to be named after Robert Moses by the City Council in 1982, a year after his death.

The sky appeared overcast and grey, but John did not despair. Instead, he grew increasingly impassioned with momentum. He took a few more jump shots and made his patented layups before heading home.

Dmitri, meanwhile, had not spoken to his friend for a few days. The corporate world dampened his soul, and John had a clear sense he wanted back in the theatrical scene. A few years already passed since *KGB Surprise*. The two met at Gem Spa later that night, and Dmitri wanted to speak with John just to know how things were proceeding with his production.

"What's new with you?" Dmitri asked
John outside the landmark magazine and tobacco
shop of the East Village.

"I spoke to the head of Madison Square
Garden, and Syracuse Stage."

"Da, you did? Nice work."

As the two shared their egg creams and
jelly rings, they reminisced for a little while
longer before retiring for the night. Dmitri told
John he was headed to Connecticut over the next
few months for "some business deal." He
underscored that he never "wanted to feel
capped," as he knew he would be getting a
promotion. He worked too hard, and was too
valuable an asset to his company for that not to
be the case.

Reality hit the two hard like a
thunderbolt, as they wished each other luck.

CHAPTER VI

'Everything went from bad to worse
Money never changed a thing
Death kept following, trackin' us down
At least I heard your bluebird sing'

On the following morning, John listened to a bootleg album of Dylan's he picked up before going to Piermont. Dylan's lyrics always had a shattering, intrinsic, and even telepathic way to play directly to his conscience at the most precise moments. His past had been "close behind" indeed, like the maestro sang with his distinctive twang in 'Tangled Up in Blue.' John read in a recent review of one of his European shows that Dylan made alterations to the song, which only added to his eager anticipation of seeing the singer-songwriter in Ireland.

John made his way to the Port Authority Bus Terminal, and he soon realized he had to take various buses to Piermont. As he got off his third bus three hours later, John knew he found the perfect spot. Set lights already illuminated the town, and John noticed a '40s-era style theatre with the blinking title that read, "THE PURPLE ROSE OF CAIRO."

"Wow, *I have arrived*," John muttered to himself.

Close to one hundred and fifty people were there, and John observed how orderly and peaceful everything felt on the set. The premise of *The Purple Rose of Cairo* depicted a Depression-era waitress named Celia, as played by Farrow, escaping to a movie theater to save her from an unhappy marriage. Celia falls for the leading actor, Tom Baxter, as played by Daniels, who literally steps out of the screen to meet her.

John unassumingly watched a few takes while standing just behind one of the gaffers for the next forty-five minutes. He watched "movie magic," as Farrow performed with Daniels and Danny Aiello. John did not notice where Allen might have been, even as his artistic presence was felt in each take. John was elated that the security guards never escorted him off the set.

The gaffer suddenly asked John, "You're an extra or something?" It jolted John somewhat, as he quickly answered.

"Just a writer. Am just here checking out another writer at work."

The crewmember, while never offering his name, gave a quizzical look. "Your moment is now, *hombre*. I can see it in your eyes. Just see through with whatever it is you're working on. It's fun. Write your book. Make your film. It's your ownership. Just hold this light for me for one second?"

"Sure."

John never felt paralyzed by the moment, and embraced the opportunity to watch Farrow and Daniels strolling down the park near the marina where they shared a laugh. He was not sure if the cameras were even rolling at the time. He marveled how low-key and natural everything felt on the shoot.

John saw a slightly built man in beige khakis with a white button down shirt wearing big headphones. *That surely was Woody Allen.* Even while given multiple opportunities to speak to Allen over the next two hours, John opted not to, never wanting to interrupt the auteur in his "element." Before he left, however, John asked the gaffer to pass along his script to Allen at some moment during the production.

"Of course," the gaffer assured him.

CHAPTER VII

John remembered that he had to return to the city to see another performance and write a review of David Mamet's *Glengarry Glen Ross*. Getting back into Manhattan at about 4:30, he made a quick stop home before making his way to the John Golden Theatre, just around the corner where *Death of a Salesman* had been playing for several months. Mamet's play already won a Drama Desk Award a few weeks earlier, including Joe Mantegna garnering a Best Actor win. John put on a VHS recording of the 1984 Tony Awards, playing Mantegna's acceptance speech.

"I must thank David Mamet, my friend – my wife Arlene, my mother Marianne," Mantegna said.

John found it touching the Chicago-based actor also thanked his friends for giving him "a place to stay while in New York."

Glengarry Glen Ross won the 1983
Laurence Olivier Award for Best New Play, and
earned the New York Drama Critics' Circle
Award in 1984.

John flashed his media credentials at the
box office. He still had two hours to spare, and
while viewing the display cases at the vaunted
theatre, he learned more of its fabled history.
These included old photographs of prior
productions, like *Waiting for Godot* in 1956, and
more recently Beth Henley's *Crimes of the
Heart*. John had not even heard of Henley despite
her play winning multiple awards.

"Here's the thing; what you do as a
screenwriter, you sell your copyright. As a
novelist, and as a playwright, you maintain your
copyright," was one of Henley's quotes, which
caught John's attention. He learned that she was
just 29 when she produced her first play. *Crimes
of the Heart* would go on to win the Pulitzer

Prize for Drama, and the New York Drama Critics Award.

"This is unbelievable!" John murmured to himself.

"It is, isn't it?" Beth Henley happened to be standing just behind him, and this made for a surprise.

"Wow, so you're Ms. Henley?"

"Beth, yes."

"Really great meeting you. Honestly, I hadn't heard much about you, or your award-winning play *Crimes of the Heart* despite being a theater critic myself I'm embarrassed to say. I do fancy myself as a playwright, too; an up-and-coming one."

"That's terrific. Your name?"

"John Duggan from Purchase, New York. I freelance often with *The Brooklyn Eagle*, and

The Daily News. I know your play won a lot of awards."

"Awards don't mean much. Getting popular can be a plague in this business. It's really about ownership of your work," she said. "You may be a bit surprised but I've read some of your analyses. I do recognize your name. You love what you do – it shines through in your work."

"Thanks so much. Acclaim doesn't help?"

"Definitely it helps, but it's really about ownership," she said. "I was teaching playwriting at University of Illinois less than a decade ago, not knowing one bit as to what lay in my future. I was at the Dallas Minority Repertory Theatre, and then onto L.A. My story is really about growing up in the Deep South. If you don't write what you know, and what you've experienced, you can't come to terms with your own past. You

can't have catharsis. Someone else will write it,
and that's death for a writer. Absolute death."

John nodded.

"I know. It's not easy. What's your play
about?"

"It's very self-reflexive. Two booksellers
in the past couple of weeks called it 'meta' –
whatever that means. I'm trying to blend in some
of my favorite creative artists since they never
worked together, and I guess the plot plays on the
fate theme. It's set in the Wild West. Granted, it's
a bit of an unwieldy narrative."

"Who are the three?"

"Woody Allen, Dustin Hoffman, and Bob
Dylan."

"Dustin's right around the corner at the
Broadhurst."

"He is, I know. I've been to a couple of
the productions, hoping to meet him after the
show, or to speak to Schlöndorff."

"And interrupt their process? That's a bit presumptuous of you, and somewhat distracting. If you're not approaching them as a critic, that's a bit intrusive."

John accepted the point and politely nodded. He privately disagreed, however.

"Is Allen shooting a new one? Just loved *Zelig* from two years ago. Definitely one of his best, especially how he got Saul Bellow and Susan Sontag as literary experts."

"Yes, *The Purple Rose of Cairo* is being filmed up in Piermont with Jeff Daniels, Mia Farrow, and Danny Aiello. I think it should be done in the next few weeks."

"Don't tell me you were hoping to go up there and give him your script?"

"I actually got back from Piermont a few hours ago. I asked a crewmember to slide it to him – just in case he may have some time to read it. It's a long shot, but I'll take my chances," he admitted.

"There's nothing wrong in that. It just seems like you're shortchanging yourself as an artist. The fertility of creativity is where you'll draw your best inspiration."

"Well, Dylan is in Europe, and I'll get to Ireland next month to see him at Slane Castle."

"Just keep plugging away on your Remington typewriter as I'm sure you've got one. Churn out what you can, and all of the details will materialize in some way. Mamet's a good one to emulate," she said with a smile. "But what a chauvinist he is! Take note how he works dialogue. He's almost like a prizefighter!"

"Indeed!" John could not agree more. "Thanks, Beth."

"Pleasure." She waved back at John, before heading down the hallway. Henley's *The*

Miss Firecracker Contest was also in production at the Manhattan Theatre that summer.

While watching *Glengarry Glen Ross*, John took notice with how Mamet used language.

"What a well-oiled machine,' John mumbled to himself.

CHAPTER VIII

John felt invigorated by his varied conversations with Irving Mitchell Felt, Beth Henley, Arthur Storch and whoever that gaffer was on Woody Allen's set. John's true moment, though, finally arrived a few weeks later as he boarded an Eastern Air Lines flight to Dublin, and made his way to the Dylan concert.

The reports were true: Joan Baez dropped out of the tour. John's mission remained steadfast: to hopefully meet Dylan to give him a copy of *Reckless Abandon*, and to overcome any lingering doubts he may still have about producing it.

His seats were good, costing him about $38.00. His flight was scheduled to land in Dublin close to five hours before the start of the show, which gave him enough time to scope out the site, in the off-chance Dylan – always a drifter – would want to speak to him.

In recent weeks, Dylan, the tireless performer, already played at some of the biggest European venues, including Schaerbeek Football Stadium in Brussels, St. James Park in Newcastle, and Ullevi Stadion in Gothenburg. Baez joined him on stage for the Hamburg, Munich and Copenhagen shows before leaving the tour. Van Morrison joined him on stage for a few shows already, and rumors swirled that he would play alongside Dylan that evening at Slane Castle. Dylan gave a rousing performance the night before at London's Wembley Stadium with Eric Clapton and The Pretenders' Chrissie Hynde joining him.

In a recent *Rolling Stone* article, Dylan was asked point-blank about whether religion defined his identity. This captivated John's interest since he found Dylan's responses to be revelatory. John was reading the *Rolling Stone* issue on the bus ride to the venue.

"People have put various labels on you over the years: 'He's a born- again Christian;' 'He's an ultra-Orthodox Jew.' Are any of those labels accurate?"

"Not really. People call you this or they call you that. But I can't respond to that, because then it seems like I'm defensive, and you know, what does it matter, really?"

"Were you aware of any anti-Semitism there when you were a kid?"

"No. Nothing really mattered to me except learning another song or a new chord or finding a new place, you know? Years later, when I'd recorded a few albums then I started seeing in places: 'Bob Dylan's a Jew,' stuff like that. I said, 'Jesus, I never knew that.' But they kept harping and it seemed like it was important for people to say that – like they'd say 'the one-legged street singer' or something. So after a period of time, I thought, 'well, gee, maybe I'll look into that."

John arrived at Slane Castle around 2:15, scouring the place in hopes of meeting Dylan. He had no media credentials for this show, and he could not help but marvel at the size of the place. He was even more enthralled by its history. He read that Brigadier General Henry first purchased the land on which it was built in 1703. In 1981, the park grounds began to host rock concerts.

John noticed an oval-shaped tent set up near the main stage. A theatrical production of Harold Pinter's *The Birthday Party* was being performed as part of Slane Castle's "Shakespeare in the Park" series. John watched as male and female thespians bickered on stage in vintage Pinteresque fashion.

Once the play concluded – John caught it about twenty-five minutes in – he got up from his lawn chair and noticed a slightly mysterious, frizzy-haired, almost diffident fellow in dark sunglasses in the front row. *He certainly looked like Bob Dylan.* The man began making his way backstage and flanked by bodyguards.

He was most certainly Bob Dylan.

Without much hesitation, John made his way closer to the stage, and shouted, "Mr. Dylan. Do you have 10 minutes?"

Dylan's security personnel were not pleased by John's antics, and began pushing him back, giving indications that he would be forced to vacate the premises. Yet Dylan, slightly amused by John's gumption, muttered to his entourage, "It's alright."

Dylan took it upon himself to approach John, offering, "Man, how can I help you?"

John decided to lay all of his anxieties to rest. "I wrote this play called *Reckless Abandon*. It's been in my head for years. I realized that you, Woody Allen and Dustin Hoffman never worked together, and thought a collaboration of the three of you would be killer. Basically, it's an odyssey that has you somewhere in the Wild West, and Woody and Hoffman are guiding you along the way, if that even makes any sense."

Dylan did not let John know what he thought of the synopsis, and gave an indifferent nod. He, instead, revealed to John that his ambition was to write the great American novel. "I still need to write something Hemingway, Camus, Dos Passos, would've found readable. I've yet to do that," Dylan said.

John was floored by Dylan's humility.

"All my songs are *just* novels in my mind. Love Remarque's *All Quiet on the Western Front* and *The Odyssey*. Their work trickles into my work lyrically, I guess. I've always wanted to know what Shakespeare was thinking when he wrote his plays. I would've loved to see him sitting at his desk, creating with his quill pen and ink. I think his writing was a form of stream-of-consciousness like how Gregory Corso does it," Dylan said with a laugh.

John could only nod.

"I've always been a fan of Beckett – that's why I'm watching this Pinter play. It preps me well for tonight. The guy can definitely write. Back in the Village, in '61, '62, I'd go to these avant-garde plays just off MacDougal Street. It ain't about plot. *It's really about moral revelation.*" Dylan then hit John with a most striking insight. "*I always admired true artists. So I learned from them.*"

The weather grew dreary and dull, and it began to rain heavily. As Dylan walked away, he gave John another bit of wisdom. "The key for me, at least, is to let your audience know it's you, but also never believe it's you." Dylan winked at John before conversing with Harold Pinter backstage. John could not help but marvel at Dylan's vulnerability as an artist in their brief exchange.

The evening's show was astounding, which included Dylan's duet with Van Morrison for "It's All Over Now, Baby Blue," "Blowin' in the Wind," and "Tupelo Honey."

CHAPTER IX

Months later would pass, and John
Duggan is seen sipping his morning coffee. The
Arts section revealed that *The Purple Rose of
Cairo* was premiering at the Ziegfeld Theater. He
smiled as he read Allen admitting that it was
the favorite of all his films.

*"Purple Rose was a film that I just locked myself
in a room. I wrote it and halfway through it
didn't go anywhere and I put it aside. I didn't
know what to do. I toyed around with other
ideas,"* Allen told the press.

Alongside the newspaper was a
paperback edition of Anton Chekhov's *Uncle
Vanya*, a gift given to him by Dmitri Ivanov who
now worked as a CEO in Stamford, Connecticut.
Dmitri also began working part-time as John's
executive producer. *Reckless Abandon* would be
their first play together as Dmitri grew inspired
by John's will and clear artistic vision. The two
men founded Chekhovian Productions, renting
out space at the Syracuse Stage over the next two
and a half months. John persuaded his friend to

not give up on his aspirations either. The Russian-American promised to write plays that largely were inspired by his upbringing. He still had his crumpled drafts inside his desk drawers.

John Duggan knew he was not Anton Chekhov, or Woody Allen, or Bob Dylan, or Dustin Hoffman, but he was his own man with his own stories to tell. He was now living with Jennifer McClure just outside Syracuse, while teaching playwriting part-time at a nearby high school. He began each class with what Dylan told him at Slane Castle: *"I always admired true artists. So I learned from them."*

CPSIA information can be obtained
at www.ICGtesting.com
Printed in the USA
BVHW031824151221
624126BV00003B/50